EDWARD

Don't miss any of these other stories by Ellen Miles!

Angel
Bandit
Baxter
Bear
Bella
Bitsy
Bonita
Boomer
Bubbles and Boo
Buddy
Champ
Chewy and Chica
Cocoa
Cody
Cooper
Daisy
Flash
Gizmo
Goldie
Gus
Honey
Jack
Jake
Liberty
Lola
Lucky
Lucy
Maggie and Max
Mocha
Molly
Moose
Muttley
Nala
Noodle
Oscar
Patches
Princess
Pugsley
Rascal
Rocky
Scout
Shadow
Snowball
Stella
Sugar, Gummi, and Lollipop
Sweetie
Teddy
Ziggy
Zipper

EDWARD

SCHOLASTIC INC.

For Rose and Edward

and for Khea, with love

Cover art by Tim O'Brien
Original cover design by Steve Scott

ISBN 978-1-338-21263-1

10 9 8 7 6 5 4 3   18 19 20 21 22

Printed in the U.S.A.   40

First printing 2018

CHAPTER ONE

"What do you think of these?" Lizzie Peterson held out a pair of pajamas to show her friend Maria. They were covered in blue and green polka dots and had big purple buttons down the front.

Maria raised her eyebrows. "Very cute," she said. "But I'm not sure they're exactly—'you.'"

Lizzie sighed. None of the pajamas in this store were really "her." "Maybe we should try another store," she said. She saw Maria raise her eyebrows again. Oh, her best friend knew her so well! Maria knew that another store wouldn't make any difference. The fact was, Lizzie was not really a pajama person. She liked to wear a T-shirt and

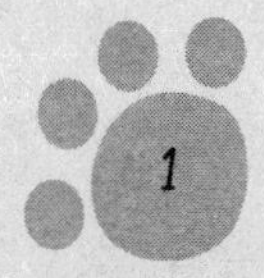

boxer shorts to bed, or a long-sleeved shirt and sweatpants when it was cold. She had never really understood the whole idea of pajamas. Why did you need special clothes for bed? Why couldn't you just wear regular clothes?

"You could just wear a T-shirt and some leggings or something," Maria said.

"Right, and be the only person on Pajamarama Day who's not in pajamas?" Lizzie asked. "I don't think so." Pajamarama was going to be a big deal at Littleton Elementary, where Lizzie and Maria were in fourth grade. Everybody was talking about it already. On the last Friday in September, everybody was going to wear pajamas to school—even the principal, Ms. Guzman, and Mr. Wood, the janitor. Plus, that night the whole fourth grade was going to have a sleepover at school.

Lizzie wasn't even sure why Pajamarama was a thing. It was bad enough that people had special

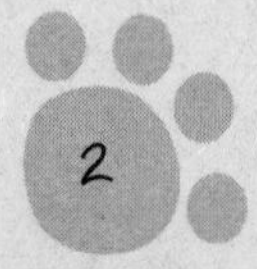

clothes for sleeping—now they were all going to wear them to school? What was the point? She sighed and put the polka-dot pajamas back on the rack. Maybe she should just wear the one pair of pajamas that she did own, the purple ones with a design of little red dogs. She'd had them for years, so they were pretty worn out and they didn't fit perfectly anymore, but at least they were "her." They had dogs on them, and Lizzie was all about dogs.

Lizzie had been dog-crazy for as long as she could remember. Besides the pajamas, she had dog-themed socks, sweatshirts, underpants, and even scrunchies. She had a huge collection of dog books and dog posters. She volunteered at the local animal shelter, helped out at her aunt's doggy day care, and even had her own very successful dog-walking business (Maria was one of the partners). Not only that, she had convinced

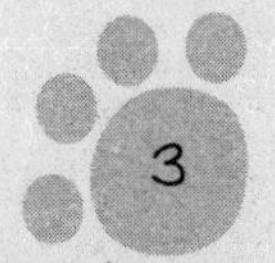

her parents that their family should foster puppies. That meant that she and her younger brothers, Charles and the Bean, had taken care of dozens of young dogs who needed their help. Every puppy only stayed a little while, until the Petersons found it the perfect forever home.

Well, every puppy but Buddy. Buddy had started out as a foster puppy, but now he was a member of the family. Lizzie loved her little brown puppy more than anything in the world. Knowing that Buddy would always be hers made up for having to say good-bye to all of the other puppies she helped foster. "I wish I could find pajamas with pictures of Buddy on them," she said to Maria now. "Wouldn't that be the best? Especially if they showed the little white heart-shaped spot on his chest."

Maria smiled. "Maybe you can find a website

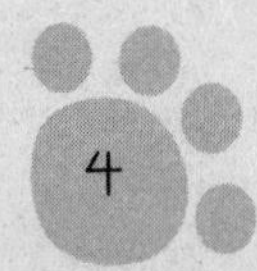

where you could get some made. But probably not in time for Pajamarama."

Lizzie rolled her eyes. "Maybe I just won't go to school on Pajamarama Day," she said.

"Oh, come on," Maria said. "It's going to be fun. Can you imagine what kind of wacky p.j.'s Ms. Guzman will come up with?"

Lizzie knew Maria was right. She went back to flipping through the pajama rack, but lost interest almost right away. "We can come back another day," she said. "There's plenty of time." She headed out of the store, with Maria following her.

They walked up Main Street toward Lucky Dog Books, where they were going to meet Lizzie's mom. The air was crisp and the sky was blue, and Lizzie's spirits lifted right away. The sun felt warm on her face as she strolled down the street. "Hi, Lizzie," said Mrs. DeMaio, who was sweeping

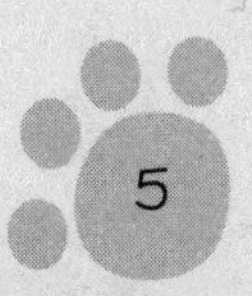

the sidewalk in front of the little grocery store she owned. “How’s Buddy?”

“He’s great,” Lizzie said. She loved it that Buddy was such a celebrity in their town. She wished she had him with her right now. Everybody liked Buddy, and she loved stopping into stores with him. She knew that Jerry Small, the owner of the bookstore, was a special fan. He would give her a big biscuit to take home to Buddy.

They passed the corner gas station where her dad had once found an abandoned puppy in a cardboard box. “Poor little Snowball,” said Lizzie. “I remember when we brought him home. He was so dirty and skinny!” He had been one of the Petersons’ first foster puppies, and once they had cleaned him up and fed him, he was one of the cutest—fluffy and white. They had found Snowball a perfect home. Lizzie smiled as she walked along, thinking about it.

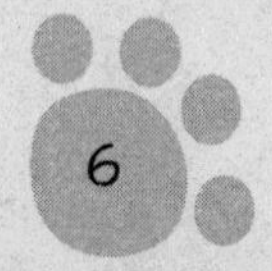

Then she saw something that made her lose her smile. She stopped short in the middle of the sidewalk. "Do you see what I see?" she asked Maria. She pointed to the yellow VW Beetle they had just passed, parked in front of the drugstore. The back windows were open, but just barely. A small black puppy stood on the backseat, his front legs up on the car door. His flat, wrinkly nose reached for the crack at the top of the window. He panted hard. His pink tongue hung out, and his bulgy black eyes gave his face a frightened look.

"Poor little pug!" Lizzie said, poking a finger through the window to pet his wet nose. The puppy snuffled at her finger, then gave it a lick. "Argh!" said Lizzie. "This makes me so mad."

CHAPTER TWO

"What?" asked Maria. "Did the puppy bite you?"

Lizzie rolled her eyes. "No," she said. "Come on, you know what I'm talking about." She pointed to the barely cracked window. "Don't you remember what it says on those flyers? Nobody should ever leave a dog closed up in a car." She pulled off her backpack and started to rummage through it. "I know I have some flyers. They're in here somewhere."

"You mean because a car can get hot if the windows aren't all the way down?" asked Maria. "Of course, everybody knows that. But it's not really that warm out today."

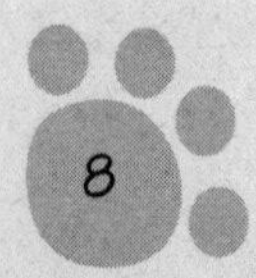

Lizzie pulled out a rumpled slip of paper that she'd printed out online. It was something you could tuck under a parked car's windshield wiper, to remind people not to leave dogs in their cars. Now she read from it. "'Even on a cool sunny day, the interior of a car can heat up quickly. A trapped dog can be in danger of major illness or even death in a matter of minutes.'" She looked up from the flyer. "I think we should call the police," she said to Maria. "This dog could be in trouble."

Maria stared at her. "Really?" she asked. "But the car is in the shade, and the owner will probably be back any minute."

Lizzie read some more from the flyer. "'Dogs don't sweat like people do. They rely on panting to keep cool. Their body temperature can rise quickly.'" She reached through the crack in the window to scratch between the dog's ears, then touched his nose again. So far, it was still wet and

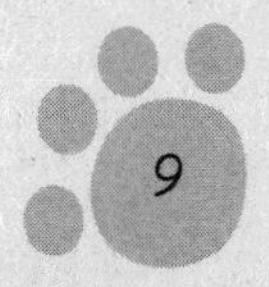

cool. "It's okay, little guy," she murmured. His flat little face was so cute, with those big bulgy eyes and worried-looking wrinkles. "We'll get you out of there." She looked toward the gas station, wondering if they had a phone she could use.

Maria reached out for the flyer. "Wait. Let me see," she said. She scanned it quickly. "It says here that if you see a dog in a parked car, the first thing you should do is try to locate the owner. *Then* you call the police or animal control."

"Okay, fine," said Lizzie. "But how do we find the owner? Do we have to go into all the stores and make an announcement?"

"I don't know," said Maria. "I think maybe we should go get your mom." She pointed to the bookstore, three doors down. "She's probably already at Lucky Dog, waiting for us."

Lizzie hopped from foot to foot. What to do? What to do?

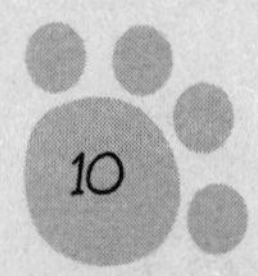

Just then, a woman came running up, waving a handful of paper towels. "Here I am!" she said. "Is he okay? I was only gone for a moment."

Lizzie folded her arms. "A moment can be too long," she said, quoting from the flyer. She frowned at the woman.

The woman rushed to the window. "Oh, Edward, are you okay, sweetie?" She opened the car door, and the puppy jumped into her arms. She dropped the paper towels and hugged him close as his whole body wriggled with joy. A second later, he started to whine—just a whimper at first, then full-blown crying.

Need my Lambie! Need my Lambie!

"Oh, you need Lambie, don't you?" asked the woman. She bent to reach inside the car and pulled out a grayish fuzzy toy that Lizzie guessed

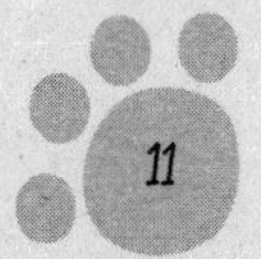

had once been an adorable white fleecy lamb. As soon as the pug saw it, he stopped whining. The woman gave it to him to hold in his teeth, and shook her head, smiling. "He can't be separated from Lambie," she said.

Lizzie couldn't help smiling back. How could she feel mad anymore when she saw how much this lady loved her dog? Still, she couldn't let the moment go by without saying something. "You really shouldn't leave him in the car alone," she said.

"I know, I know," the woman answered. "It really was for only a second. I ran to the gas station for paper towels because I didn't want him to have to sit in that mess." She pointed to the car. With the door open, Lizzie could see that the backseat was covered in—ewww!

"Did he throw up?" she asked.

The woman nodded. "He does it every time we

get in the car." She looked down at the dog in her arms and sighed. "I hate to say it, but I just don't think Edward is the right dog for me."

Lizzie's ears perked up. "What do you mean?" she asked. Maybe Edward needed a new home. Maybe Edward was going to be her family's next foster puppy! She looked around to catch Maria's eye—but Maria wasn't next to her. She glanced up the street and saw her mom coming down the sidewalk toward her, walking fast as she followed Maria back to the yellow VW. Lizzie felt relieved. It was good thinking of Maria to go get her mom. Now they could figure everything out, right then and there.

"What's going on?" Mom asked. She smiled at the woman. "I'm sorry, is Lizzie bothering you? I'm Betsy Peterson, and this is my daughter—and her friend Maria."

Lizzie put her hands on her hips. "I'm not

bothering anybody," she said. "It's this dog, Edward. He was in the car by himself. And guess what? He might need a new home."

"He was only alone for a second," said the woman, holding up her handful of paper towels. She stepped forward to shake Mom's hand. "I'm Kay. I'm an art therapist. I travel to people's homes and work with their children. I thought it would be great to have a cute little dog along with me. Kids love dogs." She hugged Edward and kissed the top of his head. "So do I," she said. "And Edward loves kids. He's crazy about children of any age."

"So what's the problem?" Maria asked.

Kay pointed to the backseat of her car, and Maria and Mom peeked in.

"Eeww," they chorused.

Kay nodded. "That's the problem," she said.

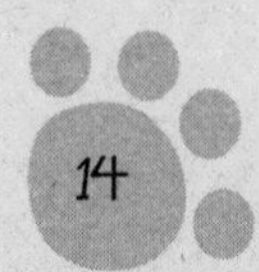

"How can I travel around with a dog who gets sick every time he's in a car?"

"Maybe he can learn," Lizzie said. "Maybe there's a way to train a dog not to be carsick." She had never come across this problem before, but she knew there was usually a solution to any dog-training issue.

"Maybe," said Kay. "But I honestly don't have the time. I'm always on the go. When I'm not working, I'm volunteering. I can't leave him home, either. I can't stand to leave him in a crate all day, but if he's free he gets up to all kinds of mischief. Anyway, why have a dog if I'm just going to leave him home alone all day? I just feel that we are not a good match, and that there's a much better owner out there for Edward." She let out a big sigh.

Lizzie looked at Mom and raised her eyebrows.

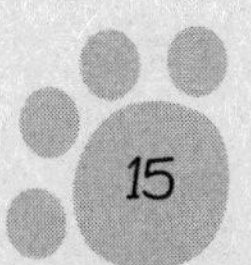

It was a silent way of saying, “Can we foster this puppy?”

Mom gave her a little nod, which meant, “Maybe.”

Lizzie turned back to Kay. “Our family fosters puppies. If you really think that Edward needs a new home, we could probably help with that. We can keep him until we find him the perfect owner.” She reached out her arms as if she expected Kay to hand Edward over, there and then.

But Kay didn’t hand him over. She hugged him tighter. “Oh, no,” she said. “I wouldn’t do that.”

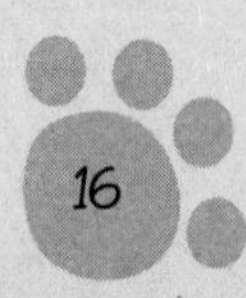

CHAPTER THREE

"You wouldn't—what?" Lizzie could hardly believe her ears. Her family had fostered so many puppies. Nobody had ever said no before when she offered help.

"I wouldn't just give my puppy up to strangers, even if you do seem like very nice strangers," said Kay. "I was on my way to an animal shelter near here, Caring Paws I think it's called? I've already spoken to the woman there about giving up Edward."

"Ms. Dobbins," said Lizzie. "I know her. I was at Caring Paws this morning, as a matter of fact. I volunteer there every week."

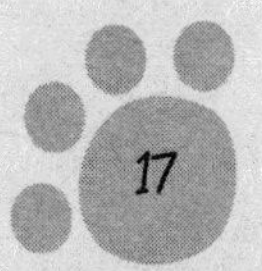

"You do?" Kay looked impressed. "Well, I suppose you do know a lot about dogs and puppies, then. But still, if I'm going to give up my dog, I want to do it the right way." She hugged Edward close. "It's not an easy choice, you know." Her voice had grown quiet as she nuzzled the pug's neck.

Lizzie couldn't help liking Kay, with her sweet smile, pink cheeks, and big pouf of white hair. She could imagine that Kay would be really great with little kids. Actually, Lizzie could see right away that Kay was the kind of person who would make a perfect owner for one of the Petersons' foster puppies. Wasn't it strange that she was about to give this puppy up?

Lizzie thought it was great that Kay cared enough to do it "the right way." Whatever that meant, exactly. Lizzie realized that she had never actually seen someone give up their dog to Ms.

Dobbins. When she worked at Caring Paws, she usually did things like walk the dogs, clean their kennels, or work on basic training like sitting and lying down. She never worked at the front desk, where they would handle what the shelter people called "relinquishment," a big word that meant giving up a pet to the care of the shelter.

"Could we come with you?" Lizzie blurted out. She was suddenly very curious about how it all worked. Did people just hand over their dogs? She knew that sometimes people left dogs at the shelter's front door, tied up or in a crate. That was definitely not the "right way." "I never saw anybody relinquish their dog before."

"Lizzie!" Mom said.

"No, it's all right," said Kay. "Maybe we'll all learn something. But first—" She held up the hand that still clutched a bunch of paper towels. "I really have to clean up that mess."

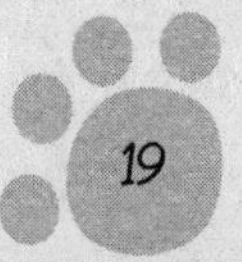

"I can hold Edward while you do it," Lizzie offered.

Kay hesitated. Then she smiled. "That would be great," she said.

Kay gently placed the puppy—and Lambie—into Lizzie's outstretched arms, and Lizzie pulled the little dog close to her chest. "Ohhh." She sighed as she sniffed the top of Edward's head. His black fur was so soft and shiny. "He smells delicious."

"I know!" said Kay. "Even after he's been sick."

Edward settled into Lizzie's embrace with only a little squirming around. He turned his sweet wrinkly flat face up to look at her, and stuck out his pink tongue to lick her. She could hear his little pug snorts and feel his warm breath on her cheek. Lizzie felt her heart swell. How could Kay stand to give up this darling boy?

"Do you mind coming along with us if we go to

Caring Paws?" Mom asked Maria quietly, while Kay leaned into the yellow VW to scrub the backseat with paper towels.

Maria shook her head as she leaned in to pet Edward. "His fur is so soft!" she said. "What a sweetie!"

Kay pulled back out of the car and tossed the used paper towels into a nearby garbage can. "He is a sweetie," she said. "But don't be tricked into thinking Edward is an angel. He's super sweet and mellow if he has your attention, or Lambie, or both. Otherwise, he can really be a handful." She held out her arms, and Lizzie handed Edward back to her. Kay kissed the top of his head and put him into the backseat. "Well," she said. "I guess it's time."

"We'll follow you, if it's really all right," said Mom.

Kay nodded. "It's fine," she said. "If I were on

my own, I might be tempted to back out of the whole plan. But I know it's the right thing to do. I've given it a lot of thought and I'm sure."

Ms. Dobbins was obviously surprised to see Lizzie back at Caring Paws. "Well, hello," she said, when Lizzie, her Mom, and Maria walked in just after Kay and Edward had arrived.

Edward strained at his leash when he saw Lizzie, panting and giving her a doggy grin. She knelt down to pet him as Kay explained the whole story, starting with how she had left Edward in the car while she ran for paper towels. "I know it's wrong to leave a dog in a car," she said. "I really do. I would never do it for more than a moment, and not even that long on a hot day."

Ms. Dobbins nodded. "I understand," she said. "But Lizzie was right to be concerned, especially

with a flat-faced breed like a pug. With those extra-short noses they can have special difficulties with breathing."

Lizzie felt herself glowing. It was nice to hear that she was right. Then Mom spoke up.

"And Lizzie understands now that she should never approach strangers on her own, even to talk about such an important thing," Mom said. "We talked about that on the way over here. She knows she needs to involve an adult right away." She gave Lizzie a look. "Right, Lizzie?"

"Right," said Lizzie. Her momentary glow was gone but she didn't care. She was still kneeling on the floor, petting Edward. He wriggled and squirmed with happiness as she scratched him between the ears and stroked his soft black fur. Was Kay really going to give up this adorable snuggle-bug?

CHAPTER FOUR

"Before we go any further, I'd like to ask a few questions," said Ms. Dobbins. "First of all, where did you get Edward?"

"From my brother," said Kay. "He had to move and he couldn't take Edward with him. I thought he'd be a perfect pet for me, but now I'm not so sure." She stooped to pick up Edward and hold him tight. "He's a darling, but I just think he might be better off with a different owner—and maybe I'd be better off with a different dog."

Ms. Dobbins nodded. "And how long have you had him?"

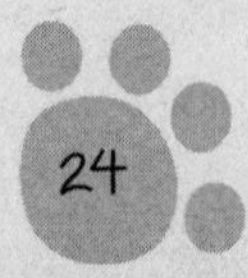

"Only a few weeks," said Kay. "And I'm already getting so attached. I know if I put this off much longer it will only get harder."

"Any major behavior problems or health issues, besides the car sickness?" Ms. Dobbins had grabbed a clipboard from the counter at the front desk and was beginning to fill out a form.

Kay looked down at Edward. "As long as he has his Lambie and some human company, he's fine," she said. "I guess when he's alone he can get up to some of the usual puppy trouble—you know, shredding things, or maybe having an accident inside. But I wouldn't call those behavior problems. He's just a baby. He still has a lot to learn." She paused and gave Edward a kiss on the head. "But really he's such a lovely pup. He has the sweetest temperament, and he loves being around children."

Ms. Dobbins leaned against the counter. "I should tell you that relinquishment is a big deal at this shelter," said Ms. Dobbins. "We really want to know everything we can about the dogs we agree to take in." She held up the clipboard. "We have this four-page form for you to fill out about the dog. We also charge a fee for any processing or veterinary work we need to do."

She put the clipboard back on the counter and crossed her arms. "Just looking at the two of you together, I am not convinced that you are really ready to give Edward up for good. Why don't you let the Petersons take him as a foster puppy while you think it over? If you did relinquish him, they would be the first people I would call, anyway. I count on them to foster the special puppies who come my way."

Kay bit her lip. Lizzie could see how hard this decision was for her.

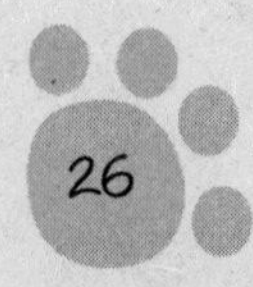

“Why don’t you come to dinner at our house so you can meet our whole family before you decide?” Mom asked. “We live very close to here, just a ten-minute drive. That way, our family can meet Edward, too. We can all make the decision together.”

Kay looked at Ms. Dobbins. She looked at Lizzie and her mom. She turned to Mom. “I’d love to join you for dinner. Thanks for asking.” Then she looked down at Edward. “What do you think, Sir Edward?” she asked.

Edward turned his face up to her and gave a few funny little pug snorts.

Whatever you want to do is fine with me!

Ms. Dobbins went behind the reception desk and came back with a handful of papers. “Here’s a blank relinquishment application. Go have

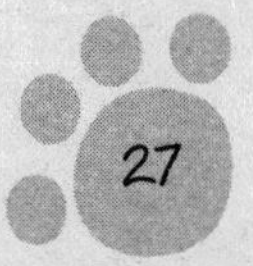

dinner with the Petersons and get to know them. Look over the form, and if you're still sure that you want to give up Edward forever, fill it out and we can talk again. Meanwhile, I'm sure the Petersons will take very good care of your boy."

"That sounds very sensible," said Kay. "But will you also keep me on your list if you come across a dog that might be right for me? I really am hoping to find a companion. A small dog, with a sweet temperament, just like this one." She smiled down at Edward. Then she sighed. "But I really do need a dog that can go anywhere with me, too," she added.

"Can Edward ride in our car?" Lizzie asked. "Maybe he's learned to associate throwing up with riding in your car, and he won't do it in a different car." She knew how dogs' brains worked. Buddy could remember the exact spot in the yard

where he once buried a bone—and he also remembered the spot where he had been stung by a bee. He avoided the bee spot, but always stopped by the bone spot and gave it a few careful sniffs, as if he was checking on whether the bone was still there. Lizzie's aunt Amanda, who ran a doggy day care center and knew everything there was to know about dogs, called that "association." She always said that it could be very strong in dogs.

Kay hesitated. Then she smiled. "Sure," she said. "I'm getting the sense that you are very trustworthy when it comes to dogs."

Lizzie grinned. "You can count on me," she said. She stood up and clucked her tongue. "Come on, Edward! Want to go for a ride?"

Edward looked up at Kay and cocked his head.

Are you coming, too?

“It’s okay, sweetie.” Kay bent down to pet him. “You go with the nice people. I’ll see you in a few minutes.”

“You can follow us if you like,” said Mom. “We’ll just be making a tiny detour to drop Maria off at home.”

Edward walked nicely on the leash as Lizzie led him out to the car. He stopped at the car door and cocked his head again, but he let Lizzie lift him up and take him into the backseat between her and Maria. He was such a good boy!

Mom started the car and pulled out of the Caring Paws lot. Lizzie petted Edward gently, murmuring comforting words to him as they drove. Edward began to pant as they drove down the road. “It’s okay, Sir Edward,” Lizzie said, using Kay’s nickname. But Edward kept panting, and even started to drool a little.

Maria held up Lambie. “Want your Lambie, Edward?” she asked.

Edward yawned. Once, twice, three times. Then he made a weird face, his lips pulled up into a strange smile.

Um, I think I’m going to—

“Mom, pull over!” said Lizzie. “Quick!”

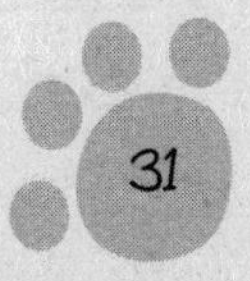

CHAPTER FIVE

They managed to make it home without any messes in the car, but it wasn't easy. Lizzie watched Edward closely for signs that he might be about to be sick, and Mom had to pull over twice more, once before they got to Maria's and once afterward. Each time, the yellow VW pulled over behind them, and Lizzie could see Kay's serious face through its windshield. Edward never actually threw up; as soon as the car stopped moving he seemed to recover. But Lizzie was beginning to understand the problem Kay faced.

"See what I mean?" Kay asked, when they had arrived at the Petersons and climbed out of their

cars. “He’s just not much of a traveler.” She scooped Edward up into her arms and kissed the top of his head. “Poor little guy.”

“It’s a problem,” Lizzie admitted. “But I still think there’s probably a way to fix it. Let’s take Edward out in the backyard,” Lizzie suggested. “He might have to pee or something, and we usually have our foster puppies meet our own puppy, Buddy, outside. It seems to work best.”

Again, Kay looked impressed. “You really do have a lot of experience, don’t you?” she asked.

Lizzie led Kay and Edward into the fenced backyard. “You can let him run around out here,” she told Kay. “It’s safe.”

The second Kay put him down, Edward dashed off like a rocket, galloping madly around the yard, sniffling and snuffling as he got to know this new place. He wagged his corkscrew tail and snorted happily.

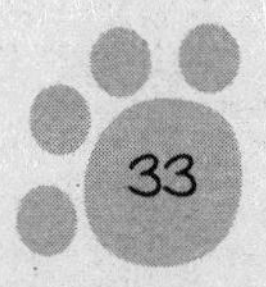

I smell another dog. A friend?

"Oh, I forgot to tell you one other thing about Edward," said Kay. "He's really, really fast."

Lizzie laughed. "No kidding," she said. Edward might look like a pudgy little stuffed animal—but he could really move.

He sprinted back to Kay, who was holding Lambie. She tossed his toy to him and he did a little pug jump to grab it out of the air. Lizzie laughed and clapped her hands. "He's adorable," she said.

"Here comes Buddy!" called Mom from the back door as she let the brown puppy out. Buddy was great with the Petersons' foster puppies. He was always friendly, and very good at sharing toys and food.

"Aww, what a cutie," said Kay as Buddy trotted

down the stairs from the back deck. "Is he one of your foster puppies? Is he available for adoption?"

Lizzie didn't like the way Kay was eyeing Buddy. She decided to clear up any confusion right away. "Buddy's our puppy," she said as she bent down to scoop Buddy up into her arms. "He started as a foster puppy, but now he's ours forever."

"I can see why you'd want to keep him. You must want to keep all your foster puppies," said Kay.

"I do," admitted Lizzie. She let Buddy down so he and Edward could run around on their own and get to know each other. "But that's not how fostering works. I just try to enjoy each puppy and then let them go."

"Very mature attitude," said Kay, nodding. "How old are you, anyway?"

“I’m ten,” said Lizzie.

“Oh, you must know my niece, then,” said Kay. “She’s probably in your grade at school. Alexandra Cook?”

Lizzie nodded. “I know her,” she said. “She’s in Mr. Fox’s class. She has curly red hair, right?”

Kay smiled. “That’s her.” Then her face changed. “Alex will be so sad to hear that Edward won’t be in our family anymore. She’s crazy about him.”

Lizzie raised her eyebrows. “Why don’t you give Edward to Alex?”

Kay shook her head. “She would love that, but her family can’t have pets at the condo where they live.” She sighed. “I’ll have to call tonight and let her know the news.”

While Lizzie and Kay talked, Edward and Buddy were getting to know each other. They dashed around the yard, Edward barreling along

on his short little pug legs with Lambie clutched in his jaws.

"Looks like they'll get along just fine," said Lizzie.

"Dinner's ready!" called Mom from the back door.

Lizzie and Kay rounded up the puppies and brought them inside.

"Uppy!" crowed the Bean, when he saw Edward. Edward galloped over to nuzzle the Bean and smother him with snuffly pug kisses.

"This is our new foster puppy?" asked Charles, kneeling to pet Edward. "He's so cute!"

"Our house is pretty much puppy-proof," said Lizzie, "so you can let Edward explore." Both puppies ran off toward the living room. Lizzie giggled. "Buddy probably wants to show Edward his toys," she said.

They sat down at the table and began passing food around.

"This looks delicious," said Kay.

"My special firehouse meat loaf recipe," said Dad. "Everybody loves it."

"The gravy is the best part," said Charles, ladling a huge pool of it onto his mashed potatoes.

Lizzie was just about to take her first yummy bite when Edward came charging into the dining room, whimpering and whining. He put his paws up on Kay's chair and whined some more.

Where's my Lambie? Where's my Lambie?

"What is it, Edward?" Lizzie asked. She looked at Kay. "Does he need to go out?"

"Is he hungry?" Mom asked.

"Do you think he's hurt?" Dad got up from his seat to check Edward out.

Kay jumped up. "It's Lambie!" she said. "He must be looking for Lambie." She ran to the living room. "Where did that toy go?"

Lizzie jumped up too and headed to the back door, wondering if Edward had left the toy outside. The second she slid the door open a black blur squeezed out past her. Edward dashed down the stairs and into the yard, heading like an arrow for a spot near the rosebushes. Seconds later he was back, clutching Lambie in his jaws. His eyes sparkled and his corkscrew tail wagged double time.

Ahh! Found my Lambie. I'm happy again.

Lizzie laughed. "We're all set!" she called. Kay joined her by the back door, laughing, too.

"Oh, Edward," she said, scooping the pudgy black pup into her arms. "You silly, silly boy."

Lizzie watched as Kay nuzzled Edward. She had to agree with Ms. Dobbins: Kay was not really ready to relinquish her pet.

CHAPTER SIX

It was a sad good-bye later that night, at least for Kay. Lizzie saw tears in the woman's eyes as she hugged Edward one last time, then turned and headed out into the dark, alone. "It's okay, Edward," Lizzie said to the soft, warm puppy she held in her arms. "We'll take good care of you."

Edward gazed up at her, blinking his big shiny black eyes. He chomped on Lambie's leg and wagged his curly little tail.

I feel safe here, as long as I have my new friends—and my Lambie.

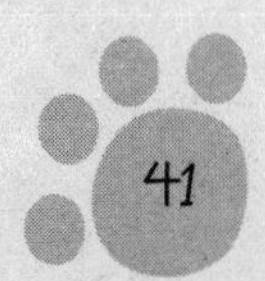

Edward settled in well that night, sleeping at the foot of Lizzie's bed with Lambie as his pillow. His snorts and snuffles kept Lizzie awake for a while, but finally she fell asleep, too. She woke as it was just getting light outside, with Edward's face pressed up against her own face. "Do you need to go out?" she asked sleepily. She carried him downstairs and took him into the backyard for a pee. Then they both went back up to snooze a little more. Sunday mornings were Lizzie's favorite: She could sleep as late as she wanted, and Dad always made blueberry pancakes for breakfast.

When she woke again, Edward was still snoring, with his chin propped on Lambie. The sweet smell of cooking wafted up from the kitchen, and Lizzie could hear her family moving around downstairs.

Lizzie lay in her bed, thinking again about Pajamarama. The whole idea made her stomach hurt. What was she going to wear? Maybe she should try on her old p.j.'s and see if they would work after all. She got up and rummaged around in the bottom drawer of her bureau. There they were! She pulled them out. She really did like these p.j.'s. They looked more like a sweatshirt and sweatpants. They were soft and comfy, and she loved the fact that they had dogs on them. She pulled off the T-shirt and boxers she had slept in and put on the pajamas.

The top was snug and the sleeves were a little short, but that was okay. She pushed the sleeves up so they looked like they were supposed to be that way, hiding the frayed cuffs by folding them over. The pants were definitely not as loose as they used to be, and they didn't seem to cover nearly as much of her ankles—but so what? They were like the capri pants everybody was wearing lately. Fashionable, really.

She tiptoed out of her room, letting Edward sleep while she went down the hall to check herself in the bathroom's full-length mirror. Charles popped out of his room just as she walked by.

He burst out laughing. "Are those the Bean's p.j.'s?" he asked. "I think you better check the size."

Lizzie felt her cheeks grow hot. She dashed back to her room and tore off the pajamas, then pulled on her regular Sunday morning clothes: sweatpants and a T-shirt. So much for her old p.j.'s. It was bad enough to have to wear sleeping clothes to school, without being laughed at. "I guess I'm going to have to figure something else out for Pajamarama," she said to Edward, who lay on the bed watching her. "Meanwhile, there's

more important stuff to do. Like—figure out how to train you to be able to ride in a car."

As soon as breakfast was over, Lizzie headed up to her mom's study. She had permission to do some Internet research, and she couldn't wait to get started. She opened the search engine and began to type "how to train a dog not to." Before she'd even finished her sentence, results were popping up. "How to train a dog not to bark . . . How to train a dog not to jump up . . . How to train a dog not to bite . . . How to train a dog not to lick . . ."

Lizzie kept typing. "How to train a dog not to throw up" and again the results started to pop up: "How to train a dog not to throw up in bed . . . How to train a dog not to throw up inside . . . How to train a dog not to throw up medicine . . ." Lizzie couldn't believe it. There sure were a lot of things people wanted dogs NOT to do!

". . . in the car," she finally finished typing, and there they were: more results! She clicked on the one that looked best and began to read.

It turned out that this throwing-up-in-the-car thing was not so unusual. Lots of dogs did it, especially puppies. Some just grew out of it, but others needed help. Lizzie read with interest about the signs that may tell you that a dog is about to throw up: Whining, yawning, and drooling were all in there, and also a funny weird smile that often came right before they vomited. "Just like you in the car yesterday," she said to Edward, who sat at her feet cuddling Lambie.

The main technique for fixing the problem was something called desensitization. "Baby steps," Lizzie told Edward, after she'd read for a while. "First we just get you to sit in the car when it's not moving, and maybe I give you a treat or two.

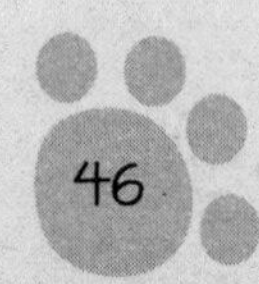

Then maybe the next day we start the car. If you can get used to being in the car while it's running, then the next step is to move the car up and down in the driveway. Then we might drive around the block. Woo-hoo!" She smiled down at him.

Once a dog got more used to being in the car, and associating it with good things like treats and attention, you could start going for longer rides. "Especially rides that end with a dog-friendly activity like playing at a dog park," Lizzie read to Edward. "That sounds like fun." She reached down to pull him—and Lambie—up onto her lap.

"I think we can solve this problem," she said as she stroked his soft fur.

Edward wagged his curly tail and snorted happily.

I'm ready for anything, as long as Lambie is along!

"We're going to need some grown-up help, though," said Lizzie. "I can't keep asking Mom and Dad to drive up and down in the driveway. Luckily, I know just the person to call." She reached for the phone and hit number three on the speed dial. After all, nobody loved pugs more than Aunt Amanda.

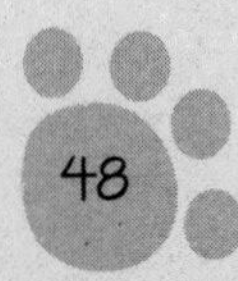

CHAPTER SEVEN

"I really think it's going to work," Lizzie told Maria the next day at recess. They were sitting on the swings, watching a kickball game. "Edward already seems comfortable in the car while it's sitting in the driveway. Aunt Amanda suggested buckling him into the safety harness we sometimes use when Buddy rides in the car. She said that the added security seems to help some dogs fight car sickness." She had already explained the whole desensitization process to Maria.

"That's great," said Maria. "I hope it keeps

working when you start driving around the block."

"I know," said Lizzie. "Aunt Amanda said she'd come help me out with that tonight. She can't wait to meet Edward."

"Maybe she needs another pug," said Maria.

Lizzie laughed. "Uncle James would kill her," she said. "After all, they already have three of them. Plus Bowser." Bowser was the big golden retriever that Aunt Amanda's doggy day care was named after: Bowser's Backyard. "But it's worth a try. After all, my aunt is the one who said that pugs are like potato chips—you just can't stop at one."

Lizzie blew on her fingers. It was chilly out, and she wondered if it would be this cold on Friday, Pajamarama. "Do you think people will play kick-ball in their pajamas?" she asked Maria.

Her friend shrugged. "Why not?"

Lizzie shook her head. "Because . . . because pajamas aren't really regular clothes. They're more like—I don't know, underwear. Like something you only wear in private."

Maria pointed a finger at Lizzie. "I knew it," she said. "Your whole problem with Pajamarama is that you're embarrassed to wear p.j.'s in public. Admit it!"

"No way!" said Lizzie. Just then, the kickball came flying toward them, and Lizzie reached up to catch it. She threw it back toward the field. "I just don't get why it's supposed to be fun." She thought again about skipping school on Friday. Would Mom let her stay home if she begged?

"Don't even think about it," said Maria, who always seemed to be able to read Lizzie's mind. "If you don't come to school that day, you'll miss

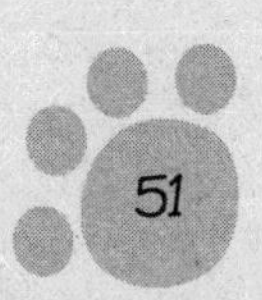

the sleepover. That's like, one of the highlights of the year. You can't miss it. I mean, what about all that great food?"

"Food?" Lizzie didn't remember anything about food.

Maria nodded. "I heard they get volunteers from the community to make us dinner that night, and great snacks like popcorn balls and s'mores. Then in the morning more people come in to make a fantastic breakfast. I heard they had waffles last year, with real maple syrup."

Lizzie was silent. Was all of that worth it? She still wasn't positive. It would depend a lot on whether she would be able to find pajamas she felt comfortable in. That seemed unlikely. "We'll see," she said, just as the bell rang. She and Maria lined up to go back to their classroom. Their teacher, Mrs. Abeson, held the door open and they trooped inside, passing the other fourth-grade

class on their way out to recess. Lizzie spotted a girl with curly red hair, and elbowed Maria. “That’s Alexandra,” she whispered. “Kay’s niece.”

The red-haired girl caught her looking and waved to Lizzie. “Hi, Lizzie!” she called. “How’s Edward? I miss him so much.”

Lizzie waved back. “He’s great,” she said. “He’s already starting to learn—” But the two classes were like schools of fish swimming in opposite directions, and before she could finish her sentence, Alexandra and the rest of her class were out the door and running onto the playground.

“I guess she knows who I am, too,” Lizzie said to Maria.

“Everybody knows who you are,” Maria said, smiling.

“But they’ve never seen me in my pajamas,” said Lizzie. “And maybe they never will.”

* * *

Edward and Buddy were waiting at the door when Lizzie got home from school that afternoon. Edward had Lambie in his mouth, and Buddy had Mr. Duck in his. When Lizzie came in, they both wagged their tails so hard that their whole back ends wagged. "You are a couple of goofballs," Lizzie said as she knelt down to give them both some pets.

She let them out in the backyard and watched them run around for a little while, thinking about her training plan for Edward. If she did a little more work with him now, just getting him used to being in the parked car in the driveway, then he'd be ready when Aunt Amanda came over. Maybe they could even drive around the block a few times.

"I think you're ready," she told Edward when he came running over for some attention. "The desensitization is working."

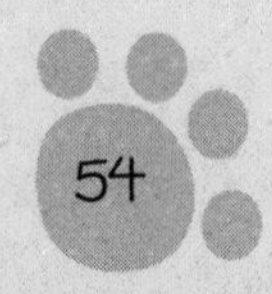

When Lizzie went up to her room to drop off her backpack, she saw a package on her bed. "What's this?" she called down the hall to her mom, who was working in her study.

"Open it and find out," said Mom.

Lizzie tore the package open. "Whoa!" she said as she pulled a pair of bright purple pajamas out of their plastic wrapping. They were just like her old ones, but bigger—she could tell right away when she held the pants up. And instead of dachshunds, they had a design of little brown dogs all over them. "The dogs look just like Buddy!" The dogs had floppy ears and white spots on their chests, just like her puppy.

"That's what I thought," said her mom, who had appeared at Lizzie's door. She smiled at Lizzie. "That's why I ordered them. They look like they'll be a good fit, too."

Lizzie threw her arms around her mom. "Thanks," she said. "They're really great."

And they were. Lizzie loved her new pajamas. There was only one problem: Now she had something to wear to Pajamarama. Lizzie felt her stomach start to clench. The truth was that Maria was right. Lizzie was embarrassed to wear her pajamas in public. The very idea made her feel like throwing up, just like riding in a car made Edward feel sick.

That was when she had a great idea. If desensitization worked so well for Edward, why couldn't it work for her, too?

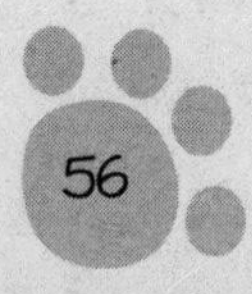

CHAPTER EIGHT

The next morning, Edward slept until it was time to get up. Or at least Lizzie guessed he was sleeping, by the way he was snoring.

Lizzie threw off the covers and got out of bed. She glanced at the pajamas still sitting on top of her bureau. Was she going to stick to the plan she'd made? She looked at Edward. "If you can do it, so can I," she told him.

She was so proud of him for the progress he had made already. The night before, when Aunt Amanda had come over, he had jumped into her car happily, and he had seemed to really enjoy

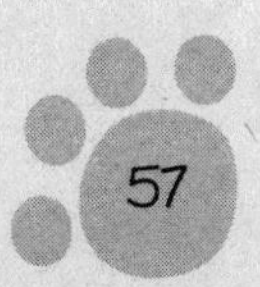

their ride around the block. "Baby steps, right?" she asked the sleepy black puppy.

Lizzie had wanted to drive farther since everything was going so well, but Aunt Amanda had said it wasn't a good idea. "You have to take it slowly with this kind of training," she said. "If you push too fast, you'll stop making progress and you might even go backward."

Since going backward could mean cleaning up after Edward—ick—Lizzie had agreed. Aunt Amanda had promised that they'd go farther on their next training jaunt.

Now it was Lizzie's turn for desensitization training. She had decided that the best way to get used to wearing pajamas in public was to start with small steps. This morning's step was to wear just the pajama top to breakfast with her family. If that went well, she might try wearing it outside of the house, when she and Maria walked dogs after school. And if *that* went well . . . Lizzie glanced at the pajama bottoms and shivered. She still couldn't quite imagine wearing the whole outfit outside of the house.

She pulled off the T-shirt she'd slept in and pulled on the new pajama top. It felt soft against her skin and it fit perfectly, loose and comfy. She looked down at the puppy print and smiled. The puppies really did look a lot like Buddy. "Okay, Edward, let's do it," she said.

She headed downstairs with the puppy trotting ahead of her. Mom was sitting at the kitchen table with a cup of coffee while Dad fixed the Bean a bowl of cereal. Charles leaned against the counter, eating a banana. Lizzie entered the room shyly, almost on tiptoe.

"Hey," said Dad. "Great top!"

Mom smiled. “Perfect fit,” she said.

“Uppy!” cried the Bean, pointing at the puppies on Lizzie’s sleeve.

“The puppies look just like Buddy,” said Charles. “Cool.”

Lizzie beamed. “Thanks,” she said. “I better take Edward outside.” She headed to the back door and slid it open, still beaming. Maybe this wasn’t going to be so hard, after all.

Still, she wasn’t ready to wear the pajama top to school. Before she left she changed into a favorite shirt, leaving the pajama top neatly folded on top of her bureau.

When she came home after school, Lizzie changed back into the top before she met Maria for dog-walking. She’d decided to surprise her friend and get an honest reaction. She threw a

jacket over the top since it was chilly again, but she left the jacket unzipped.

"Hey," said Maria, when they met on their usual corner. "What are you wearing? Is that a pajama top? It looks just like your old p.j.'s, except the dogs look just like—"

"Buddy, I know," said Lizzie. "Isn't that cool?" She told Maria how her mom had ordered the pajamas.

"So you're all set for Pajamarama," said Maria.

"Um," said Lizzie. "Let's just say I'm working on it."

On Thursday morning, Lizzie wore the pajama top *and* the bottoms down to breakfast. She braced herself, wondering if Charles would laugh at her—but he didn't. "How come I didn't get new pajamas?" he asked Mom instead.

“Because you love your dinosaur p.j.’s, and they still fit you perfectly,” Mom answered. “Weren’t you planning to wear them tomorrow to Pajamarama?”

“I guess,” said Charles. “But it’s still not fair.”

Mom shrugged. “Not fair” was never a good argument with her. She turned to Lizzie. “You look great in those, honey. Are you feeling ready to wear them to school?”

“Almost,” said Lizzie. Her desensitization training plan was working so far, but there was still one big step she had to take. She took it that night when Aunt Amanda came over to help with Edward’s training. “What do you think?” she asked her aunt, spinning around to show off the p.j.’s.

“Fabulous!” said Aunt Amanda. “I love how the dogs look just like Buddy.”

They took Edward out to the car and drove up and down the driveway a few times. “He seems

fine," reported Lizzie, who was sitting next to Edward in the backseat. He was calm, lying there with Lambie clutched between his paws. No panting, no drooling, no weird smile. "Let's try going around the block."

"I think he's ready for more than that," said Aunt Amanda. "I was thinking we could go to the pet store and buy him some treats there. Maybe even a new toy, as if he'd ever look at anything but Lambie."

Normally Lizzie loved to go to the pet store, but now she felt her stomach clench up. "Okay," she said. "But I'll wait in the car." Showing her pajamas to her aunt was one thing; going into a brightly lit store in them was another.

"I think Edward will feel more comfortable in a new place if you're with him," her aunt said gently, when they pulled into the pet-store parking lot a few minutes later.

Lizzie crossed her arms. Then she sighed. "Okay," she said. This would be a good test. If she could stand being in a pet store in her pajamas, she could probably stand wearing them to school the next day. She climbed out of the car and, with Edward trotting along beside her, followed her aunt into the store.

CHAPTER NINE

Mrs. Abeson, Lizzie and Maria's teacher, wore pink Hello Kitty p.j.'s and a white robe with a ruffle around the neckline.

Mr. Wood the janitor wore a Chicago Cubs jersey and black sweatpants.

And the principal, Ms. Guzman, who always seemed so stern, dressed in a long red plaid flannel nightie, a green plaid robe, and giant yellow curlers in her hair. She clutched a moth-eaten teddy, and a sleep mask dangled from her robe's pocket. "Ahhhh, I'm so sleepy," she said, when she passed Lizzie in the hall. She stretched her arms

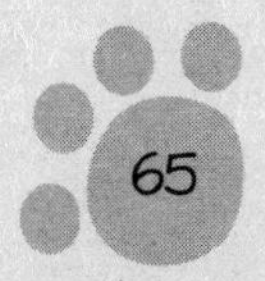

out long and faked a huge yawn. "Have you seen my bed?"

Lizzie giggled, then found herself yawning, too. Why were yawns so contagious? She didn't feel tired at all. It was Pajamarama Day and her desensitization training had totally worked. It turned out that instead of feeling weird and embarrassed she felt happy and excited. She didn't even want to hide her p.j.'s by wearing a jacket to school, but Mom had made her because the morning was frosty.

Edward's training was working, too. Last night's visit to the pet store had been a riot. Every single person in the store seemed to fall in love with Edward, who rode sitting up in Lizzie's cart with Lambie right beside him. He looked so eager and happy, snorting and snuffling and gazing this way and that with his big bulgy black eyes. Everybody smiled when they saw him,

from the clerks to the store manager to other customers. They oohed and aahed over him, petted him, and gave him treats. Edward ate up all the attention. He was a star—and so was Lizzie, in her puppy pajamas. They got almost as much attention as Edward did.

"And did you notice," Aunt Amanda had asked, when they went back out to the car with their bags full of puppy treats, "that Edward didn't seem to mind the motion of the shopping cart at all? I think he's just about over his carsick days." She held up her hand for a high five, and Lizzie slapped it.

Now, as Lizzie walked down the halls in her pajamas, she smiled at the thought that Edward was ready to find a permanent home. Best of all would be if Kay would take him back, but she had not even made one phone call all week to see how he was doing. Lizzie wondered if Kay had given

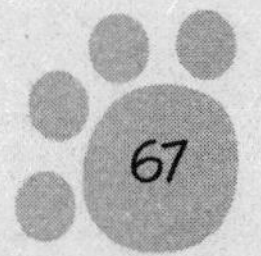

up on Edward. Had she already found another dog to adopt?

"Hey, Lizzie!" She turned to see who was calling her and saw Alexandra, Kay's niece, waving from across the hall. Alexandra wore Wonder Woman pajamas, blue and red and gold. She looked fantastic.

"Great p.j.'s," said Lizzie.

"I love yours, too," said Alexandra. "The dogs look just like Buddy!"

Lizzie stared at her. "How do you know that?"

"My aunt told me all about her visit to your house," said Alexandra. "She loved Buddy and she described him to me." She bit her lip. "I miss Edward so much. So does my aunt." she said.

"Really?" Lizzie asked. "I was wondering, because she hasn't called or visited."

Alexandra nodded. "She feels like she needs to stay away, so she can get over him. And I know

she's been over to Caring Paws a few times to look at dogs. She's trying to move on, she says."

"Oh, no," said Lizzie. She hated to think of Kay adopting another dog when Edward was so perfect for her. "Listen," she told Alexandra. "I think Edward might be cured. He can ride in a car now without getting sick."

Alexandra's mouth dropped open. "Really? That's awesome. I can't wait to tell her. She's coming tonight to bring bedtime snacks for our class."

"That's funny," said Lizzie. "My aunt is bringing snacks for my class."

The bell rang. It was time to get to her classroom. Lizzie waved good-bye to Alexandra and headed down the crowded hall. Now she barely even noticed the parade of people in their pajamas: the tiger stripes, the sports jerseys, the floral nightgowns, the truck theme, the robot theme, the plaids in every color. She hardly even saw them, because she was too busy thinking.

Wouldn't it be great if Kay happened to see Edward again, and hear for herself how well he was doing?

Right after lunch (served by the usual people in unusual outfits—Lizzie's favorite was Mrs. Duckworth's red onesie), Lizzie went straight to the pay phone in the hall outside the school office. "Aunt Amanda," she said, when her aunt picked up. "When you come tonight to drop off our snack, can you bring Edward?"

Once she had explained her plan, Aunt Amanda was totally on board. "Why not?" she asked. "He can use the practice riding in the car, anyway. I'll pick him up on my way over."

Lizzie hung up and went outside to join her class for recess. "Come on, Lizzie, we need you!"

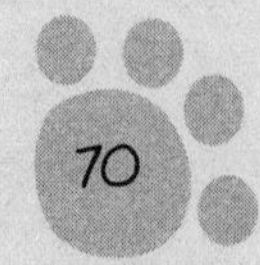

yelled Maria from the kickball field. Lizzie ran out to second base and took her position. It wasn't until she caught a ground ball and threw it to first for the out that she remembered she was in her pajamas. She laughed out loud. Her desensitization training had been a total success.

As her class filed back in to school, crossing paths with Alexandra's on their way out onto the playground, Lizzie passed the red-haired girl a note. "If u want 2 see Edward, B sure 2 volunteer 2 help bring in snax 2nite," it said.

Pajamarama Day turned out to be pretty much like any other school day, except for the fact that everybody was dressed for sleeping. It wasn't until school ended—when the last class had left the building and the last bus had left the parking lot—that everything really felt different. With only the fourth grade in the building, the school felt empty and quiet. No bells rang, no announcements came over the speakers. Then both fourth-grade classes met in the gym, and things got noisy again.

There was Sleepy Tag, where you were safe as long as you had one foot touching a mattress on the floor. Then was a spelling bee with special bedtime words. Lizzie spelled insomnia right but was out of the game when she misspelled somnambulist (Mrs. Abeson said it meant "sleepwalker," but that didn't help Lizzie figure out how to spell it). There was a crafts project where they all made full-sized cutouts of themselves to slip into full-sized paper "sleeping bags." There were read-alouds and sing-a-longs, and then there was dinner in the cafeteria.

Finally, when there was only an hour left until lights-out time and everyone had laid out their real sleeping bags on the mats in the gym, Mrs.

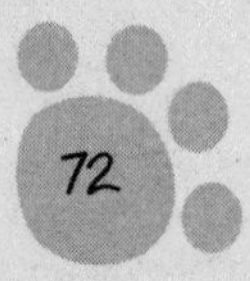

Abeson announced that the bedtime snacks would be arriving soon. "I'm guessing Lizzie and Alexandra would like to help bring them in, since their aunts are delivering," she said, and the two girls grinned at each other. They didn't even have to volunteer, after all.

When Lizzie pushed open the school's big main doors, she smiled. She didn't see Kay's yellow VW yet, but there was her aunt Amanda, standing outside her van cradling Edward in her arms.

"Edward!" cried Alexandra. She flew down the stairs and ran to Lizzie's aunt. "Can I hold him? Please?" she begged.

Aunt Amanda transferred Edward into Alexandra's arms, and Alexandra buried her nose in his neck. Lizzie stood in the doorway, grinning. She could tell how happy Kay's niece was to see her favorite puppy.

Then Edward wriggled out of Alexandra's arms and leapt to the ground. He dashed toward Lizzie, and she held out her arms for him, but he galloped right past her and ran into the school, heading straight for the noise and bustle of the gym.

CHAPTER TEN

"Nooo!" cried Lizzie as Edward raced past her. "Edward, stop!"

The barrel-shaped black pup did not even seem to hear her. He charged straight toward the wide-open gym doors and disappeared inside.

Aunt Amanda and Alexandra ran up the stairs after him. "Which way did he go?" Aunt Amanda asked, panting.

"That way," Lizzie said, pointing. "To the gym." They ran together, Alexandra way out in front. Lizzie was impressed. Alexandra was almost as fast as Edward.

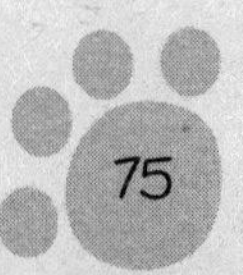

“Uh-oh,” said Lizzie as she and Aunt Amanda ran through the gym doors together.

“Ooh, boy,” echoed her aunt.

Edward was in heaven. He dashed around the gym from one group of kids to the next, soaking up the attention as everyone crowded around him for pets and kisses, then flying off to the next group calling him.

“Here, puppy!”

“Oooh, he’s so cute.”

“Catch him!”

“Come here, cutie.”

There were fifty kids yelling at once, and Edward’s excitement level just kept climbing and climbing until he was buzzing around and around the gym like a little black race car doing laps around a track.

Lizzie looked at Aunt Amanda. “What do we

do?" she asked. She could see that every time someone tried to catch Edward, he squirted out of their grasp in order to keep moving. Even Alexandra couldn't get near him.

Now the teachers and aides were yelling, too, trying to get the kids to calm down. "People! Quiet, people!" Lizzie heard someone shouting.

It didn't do any good.

The gym was in a total uproar, and Edward could not have been happier. He zoomed around, panting and happy, wriggling his funny little body joyfully every time he got a pat or a kiss.

Whee! Now we're really having fun!

Lizzie had never felt so helpless around a dog. Usually she knew what to do, but this scene had gotten out of hand so quickly that it left her

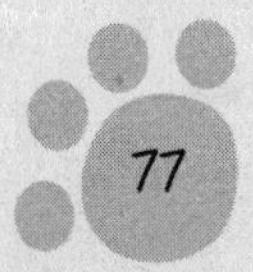

baffled. Then she heard Alexandra's voice above the crowd. "Where's Lambie?" she was yelling. "Lambie! Get Lambie."

Aunt Amanda heard it, too. Lizzie saw her sprint out of the gym as fast as she could. Lambie must be back in the van. Lizzie gave Alexandra a big thumbs-up across the gym. "Good thinking!" she called.

Moments later, Aunt Amanda was back in the gym, waving the dingy gray toy in her hand. "Edward!" she called. "Look who's here! It's your Lambie!"

Lizzie saw Edward turn to look when Aunt Amanda call his name. She saw his bulgy black eyes light up. She saw him charge across the gym.

Aunt Amanda knelt down and let Edward grab Lambie in his jaws. "There you go," she said, holding firmly to the other end of the toy. "There's

your Lambie." She clicked a leash onto his collar. "Gotcha!" she said.

Edward barely seemed to notice that he'd been caught. He had Lambie between his front paws, and his curly tail wagged madly as Edward chomped on his toy.

Where have you been? I missed you so much!

"Well, it looks as if I've missed all the fun."

Lizzie turned to see Kay standing in the gym doors, holding a tray of lemon bars.

Aunt Amanda gave Edward's leash to Alexandra and stood up. "You must be Kay. I'm Amanda," she said. "Lizzie's aunt."

Lizzie took the tray of lemon bars from Kay so that she could shake hands with Aunt Amanda, but instead Kay knelt down and opened her arms. "Edward," she said. "Come here, sweetie!"

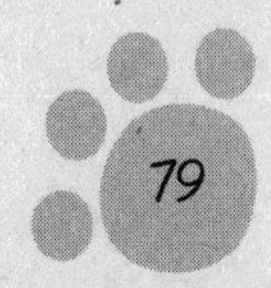

Edward bounced over to her and leapt into her waiting hug, Lambie and all. Kay kissed him all over, and Edward kissed Kay back.

Aunt Amanda laughed. "He sure is happy to see you," she said.

"I'm happy to see him, too," said Kay. But she didn't look happy. In fact, Lizzie thought she saw tears in the woman's eyes. This was why Kay had been avoiding Edward—it was just too painful for her to see him when she believed that she had to give him up.

"Guess what, Aunt Kay?" Alexandra asked. "Edward doesn't get carsick anymore. Lizzie trained him. Isn't that great?"

Lizzie held her breath, waiting to hear what Kay would say. Maybe this was when she was going to tell them that it was too late, that she had already adopted another puppy. Then she heard another voice behind her.

"What's all this?" It was Ms. Guzman, in her clashing pajamas and robe. Her curlers were falling out but she still clutched her teddy. "Who does this dog belong to?"

"He's—" Lizzie started to explain that Edward was a foster puppy, but Kay interrupted.

"He belongs to me," she said, looking down at the shiny black pup in her arms.

Alexandra let out a whoop. "Really?" she asked.

"Really," said Kay. She nuzzled Edward's neck, then glanced up at Lizzie. "I can't thank you enough for what you did," she said. "I missed this puppy so much. I'll never let him go again now."

Lizzie and Alexandra grinned at each other. Lizzie could see that Alexandra had happy tears in her eyes, and she knew she did, too. Edward was back where he belonged.

PUPPY TIPS

Car sickness is quite common in younger dogs, but they do often grow out of it. The training that Lizzie did is one way to help with the problem, and there are other methods, as well. I found Lizzie's method by researching it online, just the way she did!

It's great to have a dog who can travel anywhere with you and your parents, but it's important to consider your dog's safety, as well. Make sure he is secured with a doggy harness when he's riding in the car; always bring extra water and food; and never, never leave a dog in a car with the windows rolled up. Even if it's not hot or sunny outside, a car can heat up quickly.

Dear Reader,

All my dogs have loved riding in the car. Zipper sometimes jumps into the backseat if I leave the door open, just hoping that we'll go for a drive. But I am very careful about where and when I travel with a dog. If it's warm out, or too cold, or I know that I need to do errands and leave the car parked, the dog stays home.

Yours from the Puppy Place,

Ellen Miles

DON'T MISS THE
NEXT PUPPY PLACE
ADVENTURE!

Here's a peek at Spirit

Brrrrr!

Lizzie Peterson pulled her hood up over her red wool winter hat. It had not seemed so cold when she left her house, but that was before the wind had picked up. Now, it was fierce. The brisk gusts blew snow from the trees. Icy crystals prickled at Lizzie's face. *Brrrrr!*

Lizzie usually liked snow. When it was light and fluffy, it was perfect for playing with Buddy, her family's sweet, funny puppy. In fresh snow, Buddy would leap around, chasing and biting at snowballs. It made Lizzie and her younger brothers, Charles and the Bean, laugh out loud every time. Whenever the puppy managed to catch a clump of snow, he would immediately drop it and shake his head. The snow was just too cold for Buddy's mouth!

Today's snow was not light or fluffy. It was more like sleet or frozen ice. It left a shiny, crunchy layer on the snow from the day before. If the weather tomorrow was nicer, Lizzie would play outside with Buddy. Today, she had other plans. She was going to her friend Mariko's house.

Lizzie had met Mariko in Greenies, the environmental club. Last summer, Lizzie and Mariko had gone wild blueberry picking along with Lizzie's best friend, Maria. Together, the three girls had filled two big buckets with the plump, ink-colored berries. They finished up with a lot of blueberries, even though they all admitted to sneaking some bites as they picked. After picking, at Mariko's house, they baked blueberry muffins. It had been so much fun. The whole house had smelled delicious. Lizzie had imagined she was a character in *Blueberries for Sal*, which was one of the Bean's favorite books.

Lizzie was excited for today, too. Mariko had invited her to make maple syrup candy—from real maple syrup. It sounded like something Lizzie—and her sweet tooth—would really enjoy. The only downside was that Maria couldn't be there. Maria was training for a big indoor horse show, so she was busy for the next few weekends.

Lizzie adjusted her scarf to cover her nose and

mouth. It was so cold! Plus, it had started to sleet again—cold, icy pellets that pinged off Lizzie's jacket and stung her forehead. Even though she had gloves on, Lizzie shoved her hands into her pockets. She tried to walk faster, but the crusty snow was deep and hard to move through. Even though it would have been much warmer to ride over in the car with Dad, Lizzie had really wanted to walk to Mariko's today. She had pictured a snowy adventure, but this was turning out to be a lot snowier and a little more adventurous than she'd imagined.

Just then, Lizzie heard a tiny bark over the frosty wind. It sounded close by. That bark was followed by another one. Lizzie was sure they were from the same dog. The barks did not sound like a happy dog playing in the snow. They were sharp and loud, like the dog was in trouble.

Lizzie forced herself to move more quickly,

tugging her boots out of the deep snow. The park's soccer field looked like a sparkling white ocean, with waves of snowdrifts reaching all across the meadow.

The barks came closer and closer together. To get to Mariko's house, Lizzie needed to go left. The barks were coming from the right. Lizzie hesitated. She had told her parents she would go straight to her friend's house, but she couldn't ignore a dog in trouble. They would understand; she was sure.

Lizzie took a deep breath and trudged toward the barks. For a while, she could only see white. Then, a black dot appeared, bouncing up and down through the snow. Lizzie squinted through the snowflakes and realized that the black spot was a nose! Soon, she saw eyes and a pink tongue, too. It was a puppy, with fur so white that it blended in with the snow.

Lizzie's heart swelled as she pushed even faster toward the puppy. When they reached each other, he jumped up and put his paws on her legs. He pricked his oversized triangular ears and looked up at her with sparkling brown eyes as he yipped at her.

Who are you? Can you help? Someone needs you. Quick! I can take you there right away!

"Hello," Lizzie said, kneeling next to the excited puppy. She was tempted to take off her gloves, so she could bury them in his fluffy white fur. The puppy was gorgeous, from the tip of his fluffy tail to the tip of his shiny black nose. "Wow. A white German shepherd," she breathed. "I've seen pictures of them, but never been near one in real life. You're beautiful!" Lizzie nuzzled the puppy's neck, breathing in his delicious puppy smell. Why were puppies so—so perfect? Lizzie's family had fostered dozens of puppies who needed help, keeping each one just long enough to find it the perfect forever home—but she never got tired of how special each and every puppy truly was.

The puppy wriggled and yipped again, and Lizzie snapped back to attention. "What are you doing out here all alone? It's pretty cold, little guy." Lizzie reached around the dog's neck and found a red collar. She felt for a license or name tag, but her hands were clumsy inside the padded gloves. "Spirit," she said when she finally found the tag. There was a phone number, too. "It's nice to meet you, Spirit. I wonder if I should call this number and get you home. Do you live around here?" The puppy barked three times and then took a few steps in the other direction.

Lizzie stood back up and looked all around. She thought about what she should do. She could take the puppy to Mariko's house and call from there, but the puppy seemed to want her to go the other way.

Spirit barked once, spun around, and darted off. Lizzie didn't think twice. She followed his tracks through the snow. Even though he was only a puppy, he seemed to have a definite plan. She had to find out what it was.

ABOUT THE AUTHOR

Ellen Miles loves dogs, which is why she has a great time writing the Puppy Place books. And guess what? She loves cats, too! (In fact, her very first pet was a beautiful tortoiseshell cat named Jenny.) That's why she came up with the Kitty Corner series. Ellen lives in Vermont and loves to be outdoors with her dog, Zipper, every day, walking, biking, skiing, or swimming, depending on the season. She also loves to read, cook, explore her beautiful state, play with dogs, and hang out with friends and family.

Visit Ellen at www.ellenmiles.net.